Floppy Mop

by Bobby Lynn Maslen
pictures by John R. Maslen

Scholastic Inc.
New York • Toronto • London • Auckland • Sydney • Mexico City • New Delhi • Hong Kong • Buenos Aires

Available Bob Books®:

Set 1: Beginning Readers — With consistent new sounds added gradually, your new reader is gently introduced to all the letters of the alphabet. They can soon say, "I read the whole book!®"

Set 2: Advancing Beginners — The use of three-letter words and consistent vowel sounds in slightly longer stories build skill and confidence.

Set 3: Word Families — Consonant blends, endings and a few sight words advance reading skills while the use of word families keep reading manageable.

Set 4: Compound Words — Longer books and complex words engage young readers as proficiency advances.

Set 5: Long Vowels — Silent *e* and other vowel blends build young readers' vocabulary and aptitude.

Bob Books® Collections:

Collection 1 — Includes Set 1: Beginning Readers and part of Set 2: Advancing Beginners

Collection 2 — Includes part of Set 2: Advancing Beginners and Set 3: Word Families

Collection 3 — Includes Set 4: Compound Words and Set 5: Long Vowels

Ask for Bob Books at your local bookstore, or visit www.bobbooks.com.

ISBN 0-545-02688-1

6 5 4 3 2 1   7 8 9 10 11/0

Printed in China
This edition first printing, September 2007

Mop was a big dog.

Mop was a floppy dog.

Mop was Tom's pal.

"Come, Mop", said Tom.

Tom sat on Mop.

Jack was a cat.

Zack was a rat.

Zack ran. Jack ran after Zack.

Mop ran after Jack and Zack.

"Stop, Mop," begged Tom.
Mop stopped.

Mop and Tom sat.

Tom and Mop had a nap.

The End

List of 25 words in <u>Floppy Mop</u>

Short Vowels

<u>a</u>	<u>e</u>	<u>i</u>	<u>o</u>	<u>sight</u>
cat	begged	big	on	a
rat	end		mop	was
sat			tom	said
nap			dog	come
ran			stop	after
had			floppy	the
and				
pal				
Jack				
Zack				

60 total words in *Floppy Mop*